W9-DDV-583

Little Brothers Are...

Beth Norling

Kane/Miller
BOOK PUBLISHERS

EAST NORTHPORT, NEW YORK

little brothers are

sleepy...

spooky...

sneaky...

and short.

Little brothers are

wriggly...

pouty...

messy...

and mad.

Little brothers are

dribbly...

growly...

tricky...

and bright.

little brothers can

make up fun games.

They make you smile.

They are sweet.

They are quiet,

but best of all...

a little brother is your best friend.

I love my little brother.